For my sublime sister Josie, who is neither Mirabelle
nor Meg, but maybe a little bit of both.
K.H.
For my beautiful Liliana, who has proved herself fearless
on many occasions, except when faced with a spider.
N.A.

A TEMPLAR BOOK

First published in the UK in 2018 by Templar Publishing,
an imprint of Kings Road Publishing,
part of the Bonnier Publishing Group,
The Plaza, 535 King's Road, London, SW10 0SZ
www.templarco.co.uk
www.bonnierpublishing.com
Illustrations copyright © 2018 by Nila Aye

1 3 5 7 9 10 8 6 4 2

ISBN: 978-1-78741-073-2

Edited by Alison Ritchie
Designed by Genevieve Webster & Marty Cleary

Printed in China

FEARLESS MIRABELLE

Katie Haworth & Nila Aye

templar
books

Mirabelle and Meg Moffat were twins,
and they looked just the same.

But they were not.

Even when they were babies they were very different.

Mirabelle liked balancing . . .

Climbing . . . And jumping!

"Mirabelle is so brave!" cried their mother.
"And daring!" cried their father.
(They were famous circus acrobats so this pleased them VERY MUCH.)

Meanwhile, Meg just made
a whole lot of NOISE.

Goo goo!

He hE he!

gOO GoO!

Gaa gaa!

Goooo!

GaA gAa!

Things didn't change much
as Mirabelle and Meg got older.

Mirabelle
balanced **higher** . . .

Climbed **further** . . .

And jumped **deeper**.

Mirabelle is so fearless!

And has such derring-do!

In fact, Meg didn't try to climb anything at all.
Not even the furniture.

Then one day it was time
for Mr and Mrs Moffat to take Mirabelle and Meg to work.

In the circus tent, the twins' mother performed
a triple somersault without dropping a cherry pie.
Their father leapt from a great height
into a pool of water . . .

. . . and Mirabelle performed a back flip, leapt through six flaming loops and cartwheeled across a tightrope – seventeen times.

Then it was Meg's turn.

She started to climb to the
trapeze platform.

Up . . . Up . . . UP!

And suddenly, for the first time in her life,
Meg couldn't say ANYTHING. Her legs wobbled like jellyfish.
Her hands shook like earthquakes. Her toes trembled like turkeys.

It was then that the Moffats realised . . .

Meg was AFRAID of HEIGHTS!

Once they'd helped her down, they gave her lots of cuddles.
"Don't worry, darling," chimed her parents.
"There will be lots of amazing stuff you can do."

Meg tried all sorts of things.

Juggling . . .

Horse riding . . .

Playing in the band ...

WhAa WhuMp!

But NOTHING went right.

Meg shut herself in the caravan
and wouldn't talk to anyone.

Not even Mirabelle.

She wouldn't even come out to see
Mirabelle's grand debut. But the show had to go on . . .

FEARLESS
MIRABELLE
The AMAZING GIRL
with NO FEAR!

The crowd gasped
as Mirabelle
rode a unicycle over
a tightrope.

They 'oohed' and
'aahed' as she jumped
off and somersaulted
down ...

down ...

and down ...

They ROARED as she balanced on a galloping horse on one leg,
and ate a bowl of cereal without spilling a drop of milk.

The show was a **huge success!**
The crowd babbled, cameras flashed and microphones
were thrust in Mirabelle's face.

There was a great hush
as her fans waited . . . and waited . . .
and waited . . .

Mirabelle's legs wobbled
like jellyfish.
Her hands shook
like earthquakes.
Her toes trembled
like turkeys.
Suddenly, she couldn't say
anything at all.

FEARLESS MIRABELLE WAS

TERRIFIED!

But just then, she felt a small hand holding her own,
and heard a BIG, STRONG voice beside her.

This is my

AMAZING

sister,

FEARLESS

MIRABELLE!

And while Mirabelle **fearlessly** climbed higher and **higher . . .**

. . . Meg **fearlessly** spoke.

Look at her balancing on the high wire!

Watch
her
DIVE!

See her
SWOOP!

The audience leapt
to their feet and CHEERED
with delight.

The Moffats changed the poster a little . . .
And the show went on.

FEARLESS MIRABELLE
& MEG
The AMAZING GIRLS
with NO FEAR!

Meg is so fearless!

And has such derring-do!

Mirabelle and Meg Moffat were twins,
and they looked just the same.

But they were not.